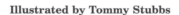

Illustrated by Tommy Stubbs

🌱 **A GOLDEN BOOK · NEW YORK**

Thomas the Tank Engine & Friends™

CREATED BY BRITT ALLCROFT

Based on The Railway Series by The Reverend W Awdry. © 2010 Gullane (Thomas) LLC.
Thomas the Tank Engine & Friends and Thomas & Friends are trademarks of Gullane (Thomas) Limited.
HIT and the HIT Entertainment logo are trademarks of HIT Entertainment Limited. All rights reserved.
Published in the United States by Golden Books, an imprint of Random House Children's Books,
a division of Random House, Inc., 1745 Broadway, New York, NY 10019, and in Canada by Random House of
Canada Limited, Toronto. Originally published by Golden Books in slightly different form as *Hero of the Rails*
in 2009. Golden Books, A Golden Book, A Little Golden Book, the G colophon, and the distinctive gold spine
are registered trademarks of Random House, Inc.

www.randomhouse.com/kids   www.thomasandfriends.com
Educators and librarians, for a variety of teaching tools, visit us at www.randomhouse.com/teachers
Library of Congress Control Number: 2009911455
ISBN: 978-0-375-85950-2
Printed in the United States of America
First Little Golden Book Edition 2010

HiT entertainment

Thomas was enjoying a quiet summer day . . .
until Spencer raced by with a *whoosh!*
  Spencer was visiting Sodor to help build
a summer house for the Duke and Duchess
of Boxford.

Spencer thought he was better and faster than all the other engines, so Thomas challenged him to a race.

Ready, set, GO!

Thomas and Spencer sped along the rails and raced around Sodor. Up and down hills, faster and faster they went.

Suddenly, Thomas' brakes broke! He crashed through some bushes—and made an incredible discovery.

Thomas found an old engine in need of repair. The engine's name was Hiro, and he had come from a distant island a long time ago. Hiro was once called the Master of the Railway.

Hiro was afraid he'd be sent to the scrap yard because he wasn't Really Useful anymore. Thomas promised to repair him in secret and make him as good as new.

Thomas found some spare parts at the bustling Sodor Steamworks. "These will help Hiro," he peeped excitedly.

But as he was on his way to visit Hiro, Thomas learned something terrible.

"The Duke and Duchess of Boxford's summer house is right next to Hiro's hiding place," Thomas peeped. "Spencer will be here every day!"

Thomas knew he would have to be careful, or Spencer would discover Hiro.

Just then, Spencer steamed around the bend.
"I think you're up to something sneaky," he puffed.
Thomas didn't answer. He just chuffed away
nervously.

Thomas couldn't do his work *and* repair Hiro on his own. He needed help, so he went to Percy and told him everything.

"Of course I'll help," Percy peeped. "What can I do?"

So Percy hid his mail cars and helped Thomas with his work. But the loads were too heavy for Percy. He soon popped a valve and needed to be repaired at the Steamworks.

Sir Topham Hatt was very cross that Percy was doing Thomas' work. Thomas didn't tell Sir Topham Hatt about Hiro. But he did tell the other engines, because he knew he needed their help, too.

Spencer wanted to know Thomas' secret, so he followed him everywhere. Thomas made sure to lead Spencer as far from Hiro as possible.

He even went out to the Quarry, where Spencer had a dusty accident.

Meanwhile, all the other engines helped
Hiro. They were amazed by his stories about
his distant home. Hiro liked his new friends,
but he missed his old friends.

A few days later, Hiro was almost as good
as new. He just needed Percy to bring one
last part. But while Hiro and Thomas waited,
Spencer huffed along the track.

"I knew you were up to something sneaky!"
Spencer puffed.

Hiro tried to race away. But without his last part, he sputtered to a stop.

As Spencer chuffed off, he laughed and said he would tell Sir Topham Hatt that the pile of scrap metal was ready for the smelting yard.

Thomas knew he had to get to Sir Topham
Hatt first. He and Spencer roared through
tunnels and rushed around bends. It was
the race of their lives!

Spencer was too heavy for the old track that crossed the marsh. With a creak and a crash, he splashed into the water.

Thomas sped to Knapford Station and told
Sir Topham Hatt everything.
   "You have found the Master of the Railway?
We must help Hiro at once!" Sir Topham
Hatt exclaimed.

After a visit to the Sodor Steamworks, Hiro was as good as new!

Thomas and Percy couldn't believe their eyes. They blew their whistles happily.

Later, Rocky, Thomas, and Hiro pulled
Spencer from the mud. But only Hiro was
mighty enough to pull Spencer all the way
back to the Steamworks. Spencer said he
was sorry for being so mean to everyone.

Spencer, Thomas, and Hiro finished the
Duke and Duchess' summer house
together. Hiro liked his friends on Sodor,
but he was still feeling very homesick.
Thomas knew Sir Topham Hatt could help.

It was time for Hiro to go home. All the engines gathered at Brendam Docks to say goodbye to their friend—the Master of the Railway.